Dear Parent:

Your child's love of reading starts here!

Every child learns to read in a different way and at his or her own speed. Some go back and forth between reading levels and read favorite books again and again. Others read through each level in order. You can help your young reader improve and become more confident by encouraging his or her own interests and abilities. From books your child reads with you to the first books he or she reads alone, there are I Can Read Books for every stage of reading:

SHARED READING
Basic language, word repetition, and whimsical illustrations, ideal for sharing with your emergent reader

BEGINNING READING
Short sentences, familiar words, and simple concepts for children eager to read on their own

READING WITH HELP
Engaging stories, longer sentences, and language play for developing readers

READING ALONE
Complex plots, challenging vocabulary, and high-interest topics for the independent reader

I Can Read Books have introduced children to the joy of reading since 1957. Featuring award-winning authors and illustrators and a fabulous cast of beloved characters, I Can Read Books set the standard for beginning readers.

A lifetime of discovery begins with the magical words "I Can Read!"

Visit www.icanread.com for information
on enriching your child's reading experience.

I Can Read® and I Can Read Book® are trademarks of HarperCollins Publishers.

Pete the Cat: Scaredy Cat!
Text copyright © 2024 by Kimberly and James Dean
Illustrations copyright © 2024 by James Dean
Pete the Cat is a registered trademark of Pete the Cat, LLC., #5118017
All rights reserved. Printed in the United States of America.
No part of this book may be used or reproduced in any manner whatsoever without written permission except in the case of brief quotations embodied in critical articles and reviews. For information address HarperCollins Children's books, a division of HarperCollins Publishers, 195 Broadway, New York, NY 10007.
www.icanread.com

Library of Congress Control Number: 2023943962
ISBN 978-0-06-309614-1 (trade bdg.) — ISBN 978-0-06-309613-4 (pbk.)

Book design by Jeanne Hogle
24 25 26 27 28 LBC 5 4 3 2 1

I Can Read!

1 BEGINNING READING

Pete the Cat
SCAREDY CAT!

by Kimberly & James Dean

HARPER
An Imprint of HarperCollinsPublishers

Pete the Cat loves stories.

Pete loves funny stories.

Pete loves bedtime stories.

And Pete really loves true stories.

But Pete has never heard a scary story.

So one cold, dark night,

Bob and Pete sit by a campfire.

"Do you want to hear

a spooky, creepy, scary story?"

Bob asks Pete.

"That sounds groovy!" says Pete.

9

Bob tells a story about a monster
with seven eyes and spaghetti arms.
The monster even has two heads
and only comes out in the dark.

"Boo!" Bob teases.

"Good googly moogly." Pete gulps.

When Bob's story ends,

Pete is a little scared,

but he says, "I love that story!"

Bob and Pete walk to the house.

"Look up," Bob tells Pete.

"The monster's seven eyes
are in the sky!"

Pete is a little scared,

but he says,

"Those are just fireflies."

Pete catches one.

When they get home,
something smells yummy!
It is dinnertime.

Bob looks at his plate.

"Are these the monster's arms?"

Bob jokes.

Pete is a little scared,

but he says,

"This is just spaghetti!"

Yum! Pete's favorite.

After dinner, Bob and Pete
watch television.

"Look at the monster's two heads!"

Bob laughs.

Pete is a little scared,

but he says,

"That's just Mom and Dad."

It is bedtime.

But it is dark.

Pete is all alone.

He is REALLY scared now!

Suddenly, Pete hears a noise.

He sees a dark shadow

and grabs a flashlight.

Pete shines the light at the shadow.

"Good googly moogly!"

"Bob?" Pete asks.

"What are you doing here?"

"I guess I was a little
scared too," Bob says.

29

"It's okay to be scared sometimes,"

Pete tells Bob.

"You are right!" Bob says.

"Plus monsters aren't real."

"Absolutely not," Pete replies.

Bob and Pete still enjoy spooky,
creepy, scary stories in the dark.
But now they are a little scared
. . . together.